VIC

D0516460

# LOST!

## A Story in String

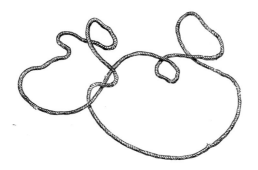

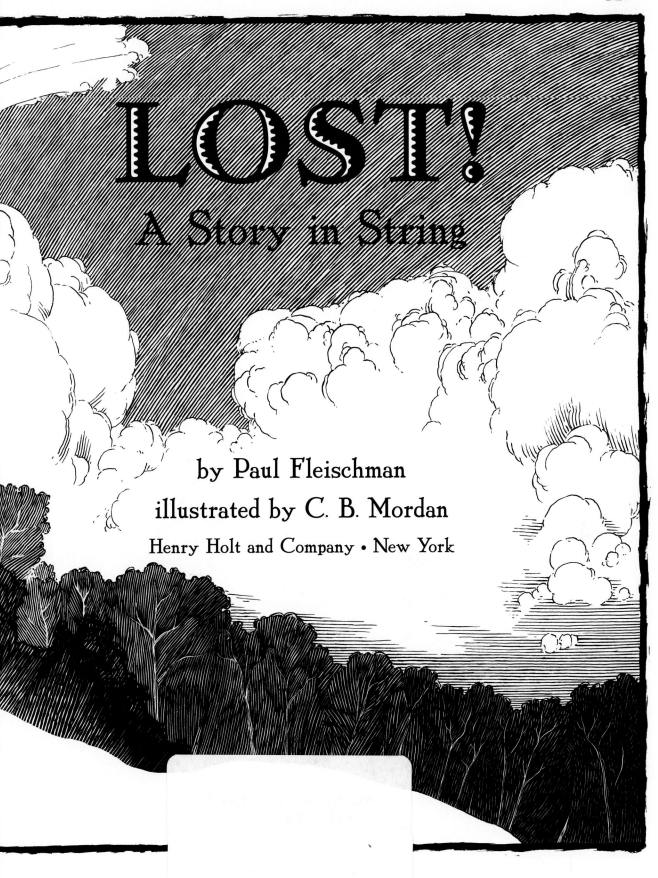

# LOST!
## A Story in String

by Paul Fleischman

illustrated by C. B. Mordan

Henry Holt and Company • New York

"*Grandmother!*"

"Yes, child."

"The electricity—it's gone out!"

"Look at that. So it has. I do love a good lightning storm. Didn't we have one the last time I visited?"

"But, Grandmother, the VCR just stopped! And the TV, too!"

"Finicky beasts."

"The radio won't work!"

"Reckon not."

"Or the computer!"

"True, child."

"Grandmother, I'll die! You have to do something!"

"You'll die?"

"Yes!"

"Gracious sakes, I could tell you a story about a girl whose life was truly in danger. A girl nine years old, just like you."

"But if you just tell it, there won't be any pictures."

"You'll have 'em. The sort that don't need electricity. A loop of yarn's all I need. Get comfortable, child. Listen—and watch."

Once there was a girl who lived up in the mountains, in a clearing you could fit in your apron pocket. Her parents tried to farm it, but times were lean. That girl didn't own one store-bought toy. About all she had in the world to play with was an old piece of string. But that was plenty enough for her. She'd twist and turn that string on her fingers until it looked like a horse or a pig or a flipper-footed goose. Sometimes she'd open the barnyard gate and bring one of her string critters inside. She'd take it to the trough for a drink of water and introduce it to all the other animals—same as if it was real.

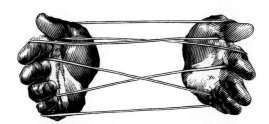

*Barnyard Gate*

"She only had brothers. They were all near grown-up and not much for playmates. So when a setter dog wandered out of the woods, one-half cockleburs and the other half mud, and took a bit of jerky from her hand, she felt like she'd made her first friend. Her father let him stay. But that dog was a roamer. The first time he left, the girl got her string and worked it into the shape of that setter, with the same long nose and hang-down ears. She was standing outside. She walked him toward the house, up the steps, then through the front door. And what do you think, child?"

"The dog came home?"

"Sleeping out on the porch in the morning.

*Dog's Head*

"A few weeks later he took off again. She made the string dog, trotted him in the house, and two days later he was back. It was November when he wandered off next. But this time the string trick didn't work. That's how she knew he must be in trouble. A man had been hunting in their woods with a bow. She wondered if the dog had been shot or had stepped into a trap and needed help. She waited five days, then couldn't stand it any longer. She studied the snow. It was good for walking, just covering the ground. The dog's prints stood out in it, clear as writing. She gathered some food, took her tall walking staff, and set off before anyone else was up—to give herself time to get back before night. And to keep anyone from stopping her.

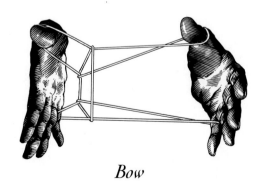

*Bow*

"It was sunny and brisk. She made good time, following those dog tracks for miles. She wove through woods and over ridges she'd never seen, knowing her footprints would lead her back home. She whistled for the dog, hour after hour, using the special whistle she'd taught him. Then the wind picked up. Clouds blew in, and snow began to fall, thick and wet. She walked on, wondering what to do. Finally she gave one last whistle, then turned around. But it was too late. Before she'd backtracked a mile, that snow had filled in her prints and the dog's. She was lost.

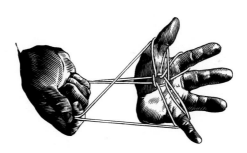

*Whistling Mouth*

"Dark was coming on. In her head, she could hear her brothers saying she'd never survive. She told 'em right back that they'd best think again. Having so much practice changing string into different things, it came natural to her to turn that walking staff of hers into a lever, hoisting up and moving a rotten log that was twice her size and uncovering a nice patch of dry ground. She laid branches against the log to make a lean-to. She was hungry, and her satchel of food was empty. She reached into her wool dress's two pockets. There was part of a biscuit in one. In the other there was half a piece of jerky. She set aside part, hungry though she was, ate the rest, and made an early night of it."

"What did she use for a pillow, Grandmother?"

"Pine needles, child. Scratchy, but powerfully fine-smelling.

*Girl in a Two-pocket Dress*

"It snowed all night and kept falling the next day. When she'd finished off the last of her food she chewed tree sap to try to hush her stomach. Then she spied a jaybird, knew it had to eat, too, and trailed it a little way through the snow. That's how she found where the hazelnuts grew. She knocked them down by the score with her staff. She filled her pockets full to the tops, used two flat stones for a nut-cracker, and dined in style that evening.

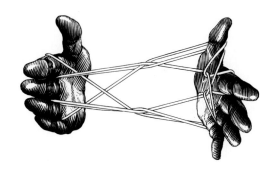

*Jay*

"That night an owl woke her up with its hooting. She could make out stars. That meant the storm was past. She'd set off in the morning—but in which direction? She felt in her bones that home lay to the north. That girl knew her constellations. There in the dark she took her staff and turned it into a compass needle, setting it down on the snow so it pointed at the North Star. When she woke in the morning the stars were gone, but she sighted down her staff and knew that north was straight toward a saw-toothed peak. She collected more hazelnuts and set off. Unfortunately, the snow was thigh-deep now. Fortunately, she was a clever tyke. With her staff, she pried two thick slabs of bark off a pine tree and turned 'em into snowshoes.

*North Star*

"She walked most of two days. When she ran out of nuts, she spied thistle tops, sharpened her staff on a boulder, and dug up the roots, sweet and juicy. She kept on toward that saw-toothed mountain. Then she heard a howl. It came from a ridge top. She whistled and the howl came again. She climbed up a hillside. There at the top, sprawled out, was that setter dog. He had feathers in his whiskers and a bullet in his leg. Caught stealing chickens, she figured. But she was too happy to give him a scolding. Especially when, from the height of that ridge, she glimpsed her house, tiny in the distance. It was dusk when she arrived, towing her dog on a sled made out of pine branches. The others were amazed to see her still alive. But young as she was, she had a heap of knowledge about getting the most out of what you've got—like making a story out of a piece of string."

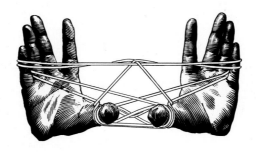

*House*

"Grandmother, was that story true?"

"It might be at that."

"How do you know?"

"Because that girl with the dog was me."

"Grandmother! You could have died!"

"But I didn't, child. And neither will you just because the power went out. After all, you're that clever girl's granddaughter."

"But, Grandmother, what will I—"

"You'll think of something, child. As for me, I believe I'll get a pinch of sleep right here in this chair."

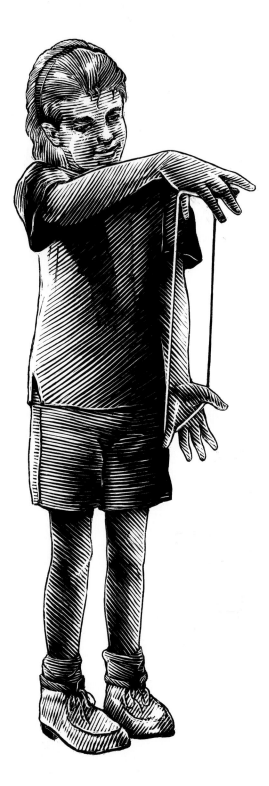

"Once there was a girl who lived in the city, in an apartment house forty floors high. . . ."

## AN ANCIENT PASTIME

Before television, before movies, before books, before written language, there was string. From the Arctic to Africa to the South Pacific, people have made designs in string to entertain themselves, to use as messages and passwords—and to illustrate stories. The Aborigines of Australia made figures of kangaroos. Eskimos made seals and polar bears. String figures were the handheld video games of their time—and more. They held mystery and magic. Some Pacific islanders believed that souls journeying to the afterworld would be asked to perform a series of string figures to gain entrance.

People are still playing with string. A loop fits into the tiniest pocket, costs practically nothing, needs no batteries, and can turn itself into thousands of different figures—including the eight shown in the story. Come learn them and take part in an ancient pastime. Then tell the grandmother's story in your own words while you create the figures. Adults will be as impressed as children.

## MAKING YOUR STRING LOOP

Earlier string artists made their loops from sinew, bark, leather, and even human hair. You'll make yours from nylon twine—thicker than kite string but thinner than clothesline. A single roll makes a lifetime supply. It's strong, slides smoothly over the fingers, and can be joined without a knot by an adult. Here's how:

Cut a piece five feet long. Take an end in each hand, let the string hang, and remove any twists by turning one end. Keeping your fingertips back half an inch from the ends, hold the string ends over a flame. They'll begin to melt. Take them out of the flame and touch them together, holding them steady. Count to ten, then use fingernail clippers to trim the joint—but be careful not to cut the string.

## BEFORE YOU BEGIN

The string figures in this story are arranged in a series, with one figure growing out of the next. Though these figures are new, the moves you'll use are common. Learning them will make it easy for you to go on to the figures in the books listed at the end. A few hints:

• Usually, you'll keep your hands as far apart as they'll go. This will keep the strings taut—not droopy.

• Sometimes the figure on your fingers might not look like the one on the page. Try moving your fingers or hands slightly. Shift the string to a different part of your fingers. Experiment.

- When you finish one figure, leave the string where it is on your fingers if you want to keep going. Each new figure requires only a few steps. If you make a mistake and need to try again, start at the first figure and work your way up to your place.

- String figures teach patience. It might take several tries before you learn a figure. Soon your fingers will be able to fly through all eight.

- In the instructions, the "near" string is the one closer to you; a "far" string is farther from you.

## MAKING THE BARNYARD GATE

*Step 1a*                               *Step 1b*

1. Put your thumbs into the loop and move your hands as far away from each other as they'll go. Now put your little fingers into the loop from below and spread your fingers.

2. Bring your right hand toward your left, slipping your right second finger under the string running across your left palm. Bring this string all the way back to the right, letting it ride on the back of your finger.

*Step 2*

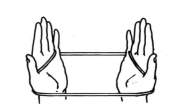

3. Do the same with your left hand's second finger. It will pass between the strings hanging from your right second finger, slip under the string running across your right palm, and return with the string on its back.

*Step 3*

4. Point your fingertips away from you. Press your thumbs and fingers together. You've made the gate! Make it swing open and closed, adding sound effects if you like.

*This string figure is actually the beginning of thousands of longer figures. It's such a common opening that it's often called "Opening A." Cat's Cradle, the most popular series of string figures, begins with a different opening, however.*

# FROM THE BARNYARD GATE TO THE DOG'S HEAD

1. Point your fingertips up. Bend your left thumb down slightly, then put it up into your left second finger's loop. Bring your thumb back, carrying with it the near string of the loop.

2. Bend your left little finger toward you, then put it up into the same loop your thumb just entered. Bring your little finger back, carrying the far string of the loop.

3. Spread your fingers wide. Move your left hand above your right, the two palms facing each other. Point your left-hand fingers up. Your audience can now see the dog, with its long nose and ears. To sneak a better peek yourself, turn your hands to the right.

*Step 1*

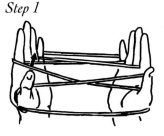

*Step 2*

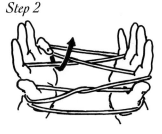

*Step 3*

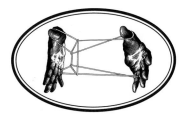

## THE DOG'S HEAD TO THE BOW

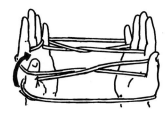

*Step 1*

1. Return your hands to their normal position, fingers pointing up. There are two strings on the back of your left thumb. The bottom string should be the one that leads to your right thumb. Your right thumb and second finger now come over and pick up the left thumb's bottom string. They lift it over the upper string and over the left thumb, then let it go.

2. Your right thumb and second finger now reach behind the left little finger. They pick up its bottom string—the one that leads to the right little finger—lift it over the left little finger, and release it. You've just learned to "Navajo" loops, lifting one over another—a move common in the string figures of the Navajo Indians. Instead of using a hand, string-figure makers often use their teeth to Navajo. Try it in step 1.

*Step 2*

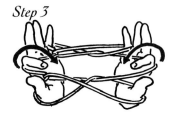

*Step 3*

3. Bend your left second finger down until its loop slides off. Now do the same with your right second finger. Pull your hands apart. You've made the bow.

*To shoot it, reach your right second finger into the middle of the bow and pull back the "bowstring" as far as it will go. At the moment you release it, pull your hands apart. You may hear the sound of the imaginary arrow flying. You can do this over and over—though the bow will gradually shrink.*

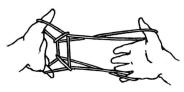

## FROM THE BOW TO THE WHISTLING MOUTH

1. Your left second finger bends down, goes up into the bow, then brings back the string that's closest to it.

2. Your left thumb now reaches toward your left little finger and slips under one of the figure's four long strings—the one that leads to the far side of the right little finger. Your thumb returns, carrying this string. The left little finger then does the same, reaching toward you over the strings, slipping under the long string that leads to the near side of the right thumb and returning with it.

3. You're ready to make the mouth whistle. Two long strings make an X in the figure. Your right thumb and second finger travel to your left hand and pick up the two strings that make the X. Get a firm grip on them. Passing just underneath these strings, your right third, fourth, and little fingers close into a fist, grasping the right thumb's other strings.

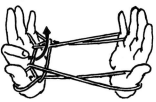

*Step 1*

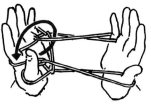

*Step 2a*

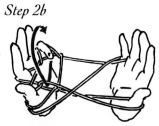

*Step 2b*

Now tilt your right hand forward and back—and watch the lips open, then close.

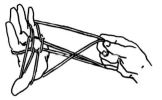

*If the mouth's hole isn't round, experiment with spreading your left hand's fingers. Grip the strings at a different spot with the right hand. Try inventing the girl's special whistle and whistling along while you move the mouth.*

## FROM THE WHISTLING MOUTH TO THE GIRL IN A TWO-POCKET DRESS

1. Let your right third, fourth, and little fingers uncurl and point away from you. Your right thumb and second finger now drop the strings they were holding. You should still have a loop on your right thumb and little finger.

2. Put your right second finger into the mouth and tug gently to the right to open it a little. Remove your second finger.

*Step 3*

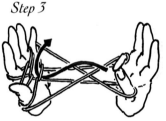

3. Bring your right thumb and little finger together until they touch. Then they travel under the mouth string that's nearest to them, tilt up, and return with that string. Let that string fall all the way to the bottom of the right thumb and little finger. Spread your fingers and point your hands away from each other, with the left hand above the right. You're finished. If you don't have an audience, get a better look by turning your hands to the right.

*Acting out the story, you can make the girl's head look down into her dress's two pockets. You can even use your left second or third finger to reach into one pocket, then the other.*

## FROM THE GIRL IN A TWO-POCKET DRESS TO THE JAY

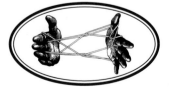

1. Your hands return to their normal position, fingers pointing up. Bend your right third finger down, catch the string running across your right palm, and lift it off the right thumb and little

finger. It now hangs on the third finger alone.

2. Using your left thumb and second finger, take the loop off the right little finger and put it onto the right fourth finger. Do the same with the right thumb's loop, dropping it onto the right second finger. The right thumb and little finger no longer have any loops. Press the fingers of your right hand together. Spread your left hand's fingers. You've made the jay.

*You can keep your hands in this position and make the jay soar. To flap its wings, angle your left thumb and little finger down and to the right. Bring those fingers toward each other, then away, keeping the strings taut so that they don't slip off.*

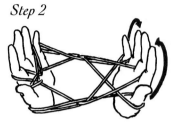

*Step 1*

*Step 2*

## FROM THE JAY TO THE NORTH STAR

1. Your left thumb and second finger pick up the right fourth finger's loop (on the little-finger side). Lift off the loop, give it half a turn toward you, then place it onto the right little finger. Do almost the same with the right second finger's loop, picking it up on the thumb side, giving it half a turn *away* from you, and placing it onto the right thumb. The twists that used to be in these loops are now gone.

2. Using your left thumb and second finger, take the loop off your right third finger. Place the loop over the right thumb and little finger.

3. Bend your left second finger down. With the help of your right second finger, remove the left second finger's loop. Pull your hands apart.

4. Each palm has a string running across it. The second, third, and fourth fingers of your right hand press closely together. Then all three of them slip under the left palm's string and return with it. The left second, third, and fourth fingers now do the same with the right palm's string. Turn your hands so that they point out from in front of

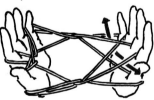

*Step 2*

*Step 3*

you, pull them apart—and look for the North Star. Adjusting fingers and strings slightly may help it show more clearly.

## FROM THE NORTH STAR TO THE HOUSE

1. Turn your hands so that your fingers point up. Reaching away from you over the other strings, your thumbs slip under the double set of strings running between the near sides of the little fingers. Your thumbs return, carrying those strings.

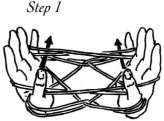

2. Bring your right second finger over the left palm strings and then between your left thumb and second finger, guiding it under the string running behind your left second, third, and fourth fingers. Lift that string on the back of your right second finger and take it off the second, third, and fourth fingers. Drop it in the center of the figure and pull your hands apart. Be careful not to lift off the little finger's loop.

3. Repeat step 2 with the left second finger, lifting off the right hand's second-third-fourth finger loop. Pressing those fingers tightly together will make it easier to remove the loop.

4. Bend your thumbs down into the opening in the center of the figure. Slowly, turn your palms outward until they face out from in front of you. You'll feel some of the loops slipping off your thumbs. Point your fingertips up and pull your thumbs and little fingers away from each other. You've made the girl's house—and brought her story to its end.

*If the house looks uneven, try moving the peak of the roof with one of your second fingers. To prevent the house from shrinking, keep a steady pressure outward with all the fingers holding loops. You can try the last move over and over by turning your palms back toward each other and inserting your thumbs under the peak of the house's roof, then bringing them toward you. This will take you back to the end of step 3.*

*For Judy Cunningham, word-weaver*
*—P. F.*

*To Linda, Caite, and Allie, I'd be lost without you—*
*and to Mr. Barry Knapp*
*—C. B. M.*

---

OTHER BOOKS AND INFORMATION

Gryski, Camilla. *Cat's Cradle, Owl's Eyes: A Book of String Games.* New York: William Morrow and Co., 1983.

———. *Many Stars and More String Games.* New York: William Morrow and Co., 1985.

———. *Super String Games.* New York: William Morrow and Co., 1987.

Johnson, Anne Akers. *Cat's Cradle: A Book of String Figures.* Palo Alto, Calif.: Klutz Press, 1993.

———. *String Games from Around the World.* Palo Alto, Calif.: Klutz Press, 1996.

The excellent books by Camilla Gryski are listed in order of difficulty. The International String Figure Association (ISFA) offers various publications, including a magazine with instructions for string figures old and new—many invented by ISFA members. Its address is ISFA, P.O. Box 5134, Pasadena, CA 91117. The group also has a site on the World Wide Web that gives links to other Web pages for string-figure makers.

Henry Holt and Company, LLC, *Publishers since 1866*

115 West 18th Street, New York, New York 10011

Henry Holt is a registered trademark of Henry Holt and Company, LLC

Text copyright © 2000 by Paul Fleischman. Illustrations copyright © 2000 by C. B. Mordan. All rights reserved.

Published in Canada by Fitzhenry & Whiteside Ltd., 195 Allstate Parkway, Markham, Ontario L3R 4T8.

Library of Congress Cataloging-in-Publication Data

Fleischman, Paul.

Lost!: a story in string/ by Paul Fleischman; illustrated by C. B. Mordan.

Summary: A grandmother tells a story about a young girl who uses her wits and what is available to her to help her survive when she is lost in the snow. Includes instructions for creating a number of string figures mentioned in the story.

[1. Lost children—Fiction. 2. Survival—Fiction. 3. Grandmothers—Fiction. 4. String figures.] I. Mordan, C. B., ill. II. Title.

PZ7.F59918Lo 1999  [Fic]—dc21  99-27997

ISBN 0-8050-5583-5 / First Edition—2000 / Designed by Martha Rago

The artist used ink on clayboard to create the illustrations for this book.

Printed in the United States of America on acid-free paper. ∞

1  3  5  7  9  10  8  6  4  2